Did your parents get a letter something like this one before you went to camp?

> *Dear Parents:*
> *We discourage care packages at camp. Please do not send junk food in the mail. These packages will be confiscated!*
> > *Sincerely,*
> > *Uncle Jay and Aunt Lucy*

This policy is an outrage! Are you a camper or a soldier? Are you here for your health or to have a good time? To conduct reverse sabotage and collect the rewards of a junk food binge, simply read this book!

SUSAN SCHNEIDER lives in Briarcliff Manor, New York, with her husband and two sons. PLEASE SEND JUNK FOOD is her first book.

PLEASE
SEND
JUNK
FOOD

A Camp Survival Guide

SUSAN SCHNEIDER

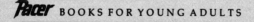

Pacer BOOKS FOR YOUNG ADULTS

a member of The Putnam Publishing Group

NEW YORK

Pacer Books are published by
The Putnam Young Readers Group
51 Madison Avenue
New York, New York 10010
Distributed by The Berkley Publishing Group

RL: 5.9

Printed in the United States of America
First printing June 1985

For my two favorite kids in the world—
Jeff and Michael
and their wonderful Dad, Eric

Special thanks to Stefanie Bromberg for
providing the perfect title for this book,
and to my "little sister" Betsy Frankenberger
for her support and encouragement

CONTENTS

GET READY

ARE YOU READY
FOR THE SUMMER?

TAKE THE CAMP APTITUDE TEST AND FIND OUT!

The summer is finally here! This means no more book reports or current-events articles. Put away that loose-leaf folder and pencil sharpener—you won't be needing them for the next eight weeks! Coats, mittens, hats and all that other stuff is gone, gone, gone. Pull out your sneakers from the bottom of your closet. Drag out your favorite T-shirt and shorts from that foreign, light-weight pile of clothes. Grab your baseball mitt, jump rope, bicycle, or what have you—it's summertime, and it's time to have fun!

Some of you may be planning to go to camp, but before your family invests in three hundred name tags, take the Camp Aptitude Test and find out what kind of camper you'd be!

Even if you plan to spend this summer in your own

backyard, you'll want to keep your C.A.T. scores handy for future plans. At the end of the quiz, add up your score and find out whether you're a *natural camper* (the first kid to put a frog in the counselor's bed), a *novice camper* (the kid who plans a night raid but gets caught), or a *hopeless camper* (the one who spends the entire summer trying to find a bus to take him/her home).

THE CAMP APTITUDE TEST

1. A J.C. is:
   a) A Jungle Crawler
   b) A Junior Counselor
   c) A Juicy Cantaloupe
   d) A Jerky Camper

2. The laundry has lost all your underwear. The best thing to do is:
   a) Call home and request an immediate emergency underwear delivery.
   b) Wear your bathing suit for the rest of the summer.
   c) Borrow underwear from a friend.
   d) Sue the camp for $21.98.

3. Your group is taking a hike in the woods when suddenly you find yourself alone and lost. You:
   a) Remain calm and stay put.
   b) Remain calm, but wander from place to place shouting "I'm here!"
   c) Get upset, cry a little, then shout "I'm here!"
   d) Panic.

4. You find yourself falling in love with a counselor. You decide to:
   a) Talk to a good friend about it.
   b) Talk to another counselor you trust about it.
   c) Write a love letter to the counselor and sign it, "Your Secret (but Young) Admirer."
   d) Read all your magazines and books for advice on romance with an older person.

5. C.I.T. Stands for:
   a) Child In Trouble
   b) Camper In Toilet
   c) Counselor In Training
   d) Camp Is Terrible

6. The camp is holding tryouts for Color War teams. You are hopelessly unathletic, so you:
   a) Explain that you think you might have a trick knee that prevents you from participating in sports activities.
   b) Volunteer to keep score at all the games.
   c) Pretend that you're really a good sportsman, but the team stinks so you don't want to play.
   d) Explain that your personal beliefs forbid war games.

7. You have developed an enormous crush on another camper. You decide to:
   a) Brush your teeth after every meal just in case you get lucky and get close.
   b) Follow him/her around camp in your shortest shorts hoping to be noticed.
   c) Take the Love Quiz (p. 116) to find out your true feelings. (Maybe it's just indigestion.)

d) Send an anonymous note and see if he/she figures out it's you.

8. The mud hole is:
   a) Where bugs are buried at camp
   b) Where you swim at camp
   c) A secret hiding place during Color War
   d) Your bunk after five days of rain

9. The best place to be on Visiting Day is:
   a) At the lake
   b) Hiding in your bunk
   c) Showing off all over camp
   d) First in line at the big barbeque

10. The best counselors at camp are usually:
    a) Young, energetic ones who are always the first on the baseball field
    b) Older ones who know what to do in an emergency
    c) Good-looking ones who spend a lot of time blow-drying their hair
    d) Married ones who spend most of their time fighting over whose bright idea it was to spend a summer at camp

SCORING
Add up the points you received on each question.

Question # 1	Question # 2	Question # 3
a = 3 points	a = 3 points	a = 4 points
b = 4 points	b = 4 points	b = 3 points
c = 1 point	c = 1 point	c = 2 points
d = 2 points	d = 2 points	d = 1 point

Question # 4
a = 4 points
b = 3 points
c = 1 point
d = 2 points

Question # 5
a = 1 point
b = 3 points
c = 4 points
d = 2 points

Question # 6
a = 4 points
b = 2 points
c = 1 point
d = 3 points

Question #7
a = 1 point
b = 3 points
c = 4 points
d = 2 points

Question # 8
a = 2 points
b = 4 points
c = 1 point
d = 3 points

Question #9
a = 2 points
b = 1 point
c = 4 points
d = 3 points

Question # 10
a = 4 points
b = 2 points
c = 3 points
d = 1 point

If you scored *30 to 40 points*, you're a *natural camper*. Even if this is your first summer at camp, you'll take to camping like a mosquito takes to a bunkful of bare-legged campers.

If you scored *20 to 30 points*, you're a *novice camper*— you've got a lot to learn, but there's hope for you in the great outdoors.

If you scored *10 to 18 points*, you're a *hopeless camper*. Consider spending the summer safely indoors at a fast-food restaurant, or a nice, air-conditioned movie theater.

Now that you know how you rate as a camper, pass the information on in a letter to a friend. If your friend is a natural camper, maybe he or she will share the secrets of success. Or if you're the pro, you can give your friends some pointers. Either way, letter writing is a vital part of camp!

Dear Jenny,

Well, here I am at Camp Na-Sha-Pa (it sounds like an Indian name, but it really stands for the director's three kids—Nancy, Shanna, and Paul). Nancy's in my bunk, which makes me a little nervous. I mean, does she report back to her father if we do something wrong? She seems nice enough, but I gave in to her when she wanted the top bunk.

I can't believe I'm here (even though we talked about it for three solid months). I hope you're right, and camp turns out to be lots of fun. Right now I feel kind of sick, and I can't decide if that's because I ate the meat for dinner (I think it was meat), or if I'm just homesick to my stomach. Since you're my best friend, I'm willing to admit to you this is the first time I've been so far away from home for more than two days, and it feels really weird. I even miss my little brother. I wonder how he's doing in Computer Camp. He won't miss anybody once they plug him in. He'll probably spend the whole summer in front of his computer trying to figure out how to screw up all the school records just like he saw in that movie this year.

I wonder what I'll really be doing all summer. Will I make new friends? There are so many activities here. I don't think I'll be good at anything! Tomorrow everyone has to take a swimming test to find out if they're beginners or advanced intermediates or what. I may die of embarrassment when they see my doggy paddle.

I hope you're having a good time. Write to me immediately.

> *Your (lonesome) friend,*
> *Betsy*

Dear Betsy,
    Camp is the GREATEST! It's absolutely wicked being a second-year camper. I'm in the Senior Girls' Bunk this year, and all the best girls are in it—Patty from last year (remember I told you about her, the one with hair so long she can sit on it!) and Donna the Dumpling. Only we have to find a new nickname for her, because she must have lost 20 pounds!! I didn't even recognize her! There's only one stuck-up snob I'll call S. She has more clothes than Princess Di—you should have seen her trying to stuff all this fancy junk into those tiny cubby holes! Anyway, I still miss you because you are my best friend for life. But I really hope you meet some great kids at your camp, too.
    Speaking of meeting great people at camp...Betsy, don't you dare tell anyone, but I think I'm IN LOVE! His name is GREG and he is too gorgeous for words!!! (Even his name is gorgeous!) He's the swimming counselor, and he is an absolute HUNK! Guess what sport is going to be my favorite this summer!
    Seriously, I've got to put GREG out of my mind (if that's possible) long enough to concentrate on my backstroke and butterfly because I want to be the best swimmer in camp this summer. I'd really like to win some medals to take home, and I think I have a pretty good chance. I want to get into gymnastics this summer, too.

Anyway, Bets, don't worry because everything is going to be great once you get used to camp. I've got to run now—tonight is the "Get Acquainted Campfire." Three guesses who I want to get acquainted with.

Love and XXXX,
Jen

CHOOSING A CAMP

Not all camps are created equal. There are sports camps for Olympic hopefuls, creative camps for poetry and flute lovers, and even slim-down camps for chocolate-chip-cookie fiends. To make matters more confusing, new specialities crop up every spring, from karate to computer camps. The trick is finding the right camp for *you*, while convincing your parents they've helped you make a wise decision.

Here are some guidelines to help you and your family make the best choice for you:

SPORTS CAMPS

If your favorite activities are running, jumping, hitting and sweating; if the sight of a soccer field or a swimming pool makes your heart pound; if the smell of the locker room gets your pulse zooming—then you're a *jock* and you belong in *sports camp*.

Sports camps teach you to pitch a curve ball and kick a field goal rather than sit in the hot sun stringing beads. At sports camp you wolf down burgers and gallons of milk as you run your tootsies off from sunup to sundown. Your counselors have names like Slugger, Coach and Killer (this includes the girls). They are friendly and simple, and sleep so soundly that even after lights out they don't hear all the talking going on.

There are baseball camps, soccer camps, swimming camps, football camps, tennis camps, jogging camps, and even pigeon-toed Ping-Pong camps (beware: this camp is full of birdbrains!).

ARTSY-CRAFTSY CAMPS

The direct opposite of sports camp is an *artsy-craftsy camp*. These camps draw a lot of kids from artsy cities like New York, Boston and San Francisco. The term "hippie" is often still used to describe the campers and counselors at this kind of camp.

The kids are unconventional, intellectual types who have two pairs of glasses and quote poetry for fun. The counselors are an interesting mix of quiet, deep thinkers who eat yogurt and bean curd, and flamboyant nuts who wear purple, orange and yellow shirts and high-top sneakers. Activities at these "explore-your-inner-self" camps include drama, dance, writing, music (classical, jazz, and folk) and art. Some *really* progressive camps have nude animal drawing classes.

If you always wanted to go to a school like the one in the TV show *Fame,* an *artsy-craftsy camp* is the place for you. (Your parents don't have to be ex—flower children for you to attend).

RICH KIDS CAMP

You were born with a silver rattle in your fist, and your first words were "charge it." Your Sweet-Sixteen party will be catered. Let's face it—you're *rich*. You wouldn't want to go to a camp without maid service!

Rich kids camps are easy to spot from the crest on their letterhead to the price of their summer season. Camp directors have names like Skip and Millicent Johnston, or Roddy and Buffy Bluestone III. Children are "bussed" to camp in air-conditioned limousines. "Bunks" consist of carpeted cottages with an oil painting of the camp director's cocker spaniel. The mess hall is referred to as the "Hunting Lodge," and there is the "Club Room" instead of a canteen.

Life at *Rich kids camp* is soft and full of social graces. Wake-up is at noon, followed by afternoon activities: horseback riding on the beach, learning how to eat without scraping the silverware against your teeth, polo, waterskiing and squash. Sweating is prohibited. Tea is at four.

WORK CAMPS, Y CAMPS, and SCOUT CAMPS

Work, Y and scout camps have several traits in common: they're rough, they're tough, they're real campin' stuff (and popular with parents, because they cost less than a swimming pool in the backyard). These camps promise to turn any kid into a *real worker*, a *real trouper*, or a *real fitness nut* who will play volleyball at the Y for the rest of his or her life.

One of the best features of these camps is their beautiful location in the wilderness. Tall, mosquito-infested reeds billowing in the wind, birds gayly singing at six o'clock in the morning. If you love the outdoors, all kinds of water sports, hiking in 90-degree weather with a pack on your back, and the idea of *real* camping in the woods—this is the kind of camp for you. (If you're only a two-weeker at a scout camp, you can count on surviving even if you never learn how to make a campfire without matches!)

COMPUTER CAMPS

If you can explain the difference between software and hardware, know logo from Pascal, and wouldn't think of taking a "byte" from your Apple—then you belong in *Computer camp!*

Computer camps have multiplied like microchips ever since the personal-computer craze began sweeping the nation. These camps are known for their exotic equipment, brainy counselors, and creative approach to camp schedules. (You can spend up to eight hours a day in front of a glowing green screen. The only setback is your inability to comprehend the English language unless it is placed before you on a data sheet.)

Computer camps cost more than work camps, but parents relax, knowing their son or daughter will return to school completely "computer literate" and with training that is readying you for the career of the future!

You'll never find the ideal camp, but each camp has its own special fun. To broaden your "camp" experience, choose one type of camp this year and next year try someplace else!

Dear Doug,

Our English teacher will never believe that I'm actually writing you a letter. But here goes. Just don't correct my spelling!

Today we took our first hike in the woods. The first few days we spent getting settled in and meeting the new kids at camp. There's this guy in my tent who's really into backpacking. He brought all his camping gear and unloaded it in the middle of the tent. I thought helping him put his stuff away was going to take the entire summer! Boy, did he have some great fishing rods and sinkers. I can't wait to go out on the lake and catch some perch. I don't think there's anything I like more than fresh fish barbequed on an open fire.

Well anyway, we only hiked two or three trails. Most of the guys were able to keep up, but that's not saying a whole lot since all the paths were cleared.

How's camp going for you? Write and let me know.

Mitch

Dear Mitch,

Baseball camp is terrific! Every day I wake up, stretch out for an hour or so, and the rest of the day we spend on the field. The counselors here are real pros. They all have positions on their teams at college. At the end of the day we warm down with an easy jog around the lake. The air is so fresh here, nothing like the fumes we breathe back home.

I've been working a lot on my pitching arm—it's looking real good. Our first game is against this neighboring camp. I heard they're no competition. We've slaughtered them five years in a row!

Friday night is our first camp social with the girls' camp across the lake. I guess it's going to be a dance

or game night or something like that. I'll let you know
what happens.

> Your buddy,
> Doug

PREPARING FOR DEPARTURE

Before you begin packing for camp, you've got to consider what kind of Mom, Dad, or other parent figure you've got living with you.

Find the description below that best fits *your* parents.

Type A Parents:—SUPERMOM/SUPERDAD

Is there a pad of paper, a ball-point pen and a list of emergency numbers by every telephone in your house? Do you have enough cans of food in your kitchen to survive a blizzard, a blackout, or a nuclear accident? Is your underwear ironed and folded when it appears in your drawers?

Consider yourself lucky to be living with a Supermom or Superdad. Your name tags will be ordered in December, along with warm blankets, pajamas, and fourteen pairs of underwear. Everything you need for camp will be labeled, washed, ironed and packed by

March 1. Your Supermom or Superdad will probably even provide postcards and letters (preaddressed and stamped) so their Superkid will never forget to write home. Rest easy. You're ready for camp; hope the rest of the summer will be so good!

Type B Parents:—SLOPPY MOM/SLOPPY DAD

If dirty socks seem a natural part of the bedroom decor; if the laundry is never starched, bleached or sorted; if they do their grocery shopping at 11 P.M. and break out in hives when asked to join a car pool, you're living with a Sloppy Mom or Dad, whose idea of a hot meal is canned ravioli! The sight of a camp list makes them paranoid—they know they're going to *lose* the list as soon as they get it, anyway! So, if you've got a Sloppy Mom or Dad at home, don't despair. There are several ways you can help them get you ready for camp:

Tell them if they *don't* take you shopping by May 1 you will *not* be able to go to camp, and they will be stuck with you all summer. This means more loads of laundry and extra trips to the grocery store.

Buy a permanent marker instead of name tags to help save time. But make sure *you* write your name in your clothes, otherwise you may not be able to read your Sloppy Parents' sloppy handwriting.

Take an older brother or sister and a credit card on a shopping spree. Leave Mom and Dad at home watching TV and losing peanut shells under the sofa.

BUYING YOUR WARDROBE, OR HOW TO DRESS LIKE AN EXPERIENCED CAMPER

Certain clothes go with camp like peanut butter with jelly. T-shirts, shorts and cut-off jeans are always in good camp spirit. Sandals, sneakers and rubber thongs that go squoosh are even better. The noisier you are, the more attention you'll get! Some campers love thongs so much they hang miniature, rainbow ones from their key chains.

Most camps mail you a camp-clothing list to let you know how many pairs of socks, underwear and pajamas you need. And in the morning, after they blow reveille, the camp director will announce the weather for that day and tell the small kids what to wear!

The camp-clothing list is a handy guide to the bare necessities of clothing for camp. But not if you're a fashion-conscious camper. If you want to know how to camp out in style, follow these pointers:

T-SHIRTS

T-shirts are the backbone of your camp wardrobe. Funky, silly and weird ones are always great to wear at camp. Nowhere else but in camp do people respect the classic T-shirt. T-shirts with pictures of your favorite rock group or singer are always the coolest ones, unless you have a T-shirt with an original air-brushed design on it.

But if you don't have one of those, brightly colored T-shirts with pictures and sayings, which have been washed a zillion times, are the best. They're comfortable and fun for all camp activities. And if you're a slob, they're even better. You can spill half your lunch right on your T-shirt, and no one will even notice!

DRESSY T-SHIRTS FOR EVENING

It's always a good idea to bring three of four classic, good-looking T-shirts to camp. Some prefer the ones with real collars and animal insignia sewn on the chest. Try to keep your "good" T-shirts clean for special occasions like camp socials.

Your camp may have its own T-shirt, which you'll probably buy. Usually it's the counselors and the young campers who wear these shirts in the interest of good camp spirit. But camp T-shirts are fun to wear in September, when you can wear them back to school.

SHORTS

What goes better with T-shirts than lots of cool, comfortable shorts? Nothing. That's why it's just as important to have cool shorts as it is to have shirts. Comfortable shorts are a must! Gym shorts with elasticized waists are always good. But because they're so popular, choose zany colors to stand out in the crowd!

Maybe dazzling yellow, orange or pink. Purple shorts for guys always go over big at camp! Make sure your shorts are roomy enough for any camp activity. And, for boys, save room in the duffle bag because extra shorts can double as swimming trunks.

JEANS

Jeans are great at camp. Where else does wearing a pair of jeans count as "dressing up"? There are different kinds of jeans for different kinds of activities. Ragged-out jeans are for horseback riding or just hanging out. To evening socials, the designer jean takes first place. One word of caution: Never, *never* wear tight jeans to a punk or rock dance. They just don't provide enough room for the right movements!

SWEAT SHIRTS / SWEAT PANTS / SWEAT SUITS

You'll do a lot of sweating at camp if you wear sweat suits in the sun. So save them for playing games, participating in sports and athletics, and keeping warm at night. They feel terrific to climb into after a cool shower or a swim in the lake. Try to keep the sweat style simple. Lots of buttons, zippers, and metal thingamajigs fall off and break at camp. Plain, hooded sweat shirts are usually the most comfortable and practical. Without TV or radio, you never know when it's going to rain at camp!

BATHING SUITS

Boys generally wear bathing suits at camp for two major purposes—swimming and attracting girls. Girls wear their bathing suits for the same reasons. For a guy, the ideal bathing suit is usually a worn-out pair of cut-offs. It's easy for a guy, because their shorts can look

great and wear well at the same time. Not so for girls
The sexy swimsuit is good for the tan, but worthles
in the water.

Important Note: If you're not happy with the way yo
look in a bathing suit, start swimming! A good bathin
suit and a good swimmer are made for each other. Sac
rifice style and buy a practical bathing suit that wil
allow you to stretch comfortably in the water. In n
time at all, you and your bathing suit will be a hit a
the docks!

PAJAMAS

The right pajamas can make a camp evening perfec
Snuggling up in warm, soft pajamas with a bunk win
dow open to let in the fresh air are the two foremos
ingredients for a perfect camp night. Draw the blanke
around your ears and tuck your feet under to stay warn
the entire night. And in case your bunk gets raided b
members of the opposite sex—you'll look great!

UNDERWEAR

Last (but not least) is the stuff that goes on first—
your underwear. Again, your major consideration her
is comfort. Choose light-weight, easy-to-wash unde
wear that fits well. Bring lots of underwear to camp
because camp laundries like to eat more underwea
than any other kind of clothing, except socks. And don
embarrass yourself by bringing your oldest, grungies
underwear, because everyone sees you—even if you tr
to hide in the bathroom when changing.

SAYING GOODBYE

Whether you leave by plane, train, car or bus, saying goodbye is always the hardest part of going to camp. But don't worry—every *other* kid is just as embarrassed watching his grown parents cry! Fathers are usually the worst; the bigger they are, the harder they blow their noses.

You can help your parents through this difficult time by being mature and understanding. Help ease the pain of separation. Say quietly:

"Mom, remember that camp is a growing experience. By the end of the summer, I'm sure I'll be much taller."

"You can use my bike when I'm gone, Dad. Also the VCR, Atari, and Apple computer. If you promise to be careful, I'll even let you drive the Corvette."

"Think of it this way, Mom. No more dirty socks or sticky counters."

"I'll miss you too, Dad, but you're not losing a son—

31

you're gaining eight totally quiet, peaceful, uninter-
rupted weekends."

Now give your parents a kiss and a hug and leave
rapidly. *Do not look back*. Parents are suckers for a
sloppy goodbye. (Don't forget, you'll be seeing them by
the end of the summer.)

THE BUS TRIP, OR GETTING THERE IS HALF THE FUN

The bus ride can be really fun. You say goodbye to your folks and hello to all the kids who will now comprise your new family. The feeling of camaraderie is expressed by the giving and receiving of tidbits of food. If someone is willing to share any kind of junk food or treat, then you know you're on the way to making a friend.

You'll want to make a good first impression on this important trip. What you wear, what you say, what you bring, and even what you eat on the bus can mark the difference between starting off on the right foot or putting your foot in your mouth (acceptable only at Gymnastics Camp).

Here are some bus do's and don'ts:

WHAT TO WEAR
1. Dress casually and comfortably. Running shorts, T-shirts and loose jeans are best. Be prepared to

sweat, stretch, bend and belch. Tight pants may look good, but they're going to feel awful when the next rest stop is more than an hour away.

2. Don't bring a Walkman on the bus unless you have two sets of headphones for sharing. A popular tape may sound good, but you don't want it to be your only friend at camp!

3. Wear sneakers or sandals. They're good for the feet. Avoid clogs, wedgies and high-heeled shoes (dangerous when getting on and off a bus, and they can inhibit spontaneous activities).

WHAT TO BRING

1. Magazines and paperback books are good to bring if you need time to adjust to your new environment. You can read until you feel comfortable enough to make conversation.

2. Gum and breath mints. Good to keep your mouth busy, great to share—and they take the worry out of getting close to new kids!

3. Junk food—candy bars, Cracker Jack, jawbreakers. Get your licks in now, because you may have to go cold turkey until you get your first care package from home.

WHAT TO EAT

Food is useful on a long bus trip for many reasons. You can eat it if you're hungry or share it to be friendly. (Hint: If you find out in advance that your counselor is on the bus, don't start a food fight.)

Supermoms or Superdads will be sure to pack a special lunch for their kids. They'll have everything neatly wrapped and labeled so eating remains a simple task and doesn't add to the confusion of being a new camper.

A Sloppy Mom or Dad will pack whatever is left over from last night's dinner. Usually these lunches are the most exotic, even if they don't taste half as good as they look!

To avoid spilling or dropping your food and looking like a slob, here is a list of *safe* foods to bring on the bus:

1. Cold chicken
2. Sandwiches like peanut butter and jelly, roast beef, turkey or bologna
3. Hard fruit (as opposed to soft fruit, which squishes when you sit on it)
4. Cookies, brownies, Twinkies and fruit pies
5. Anything Grandma made for you

WHAT TO SAY

Conversation is rarely a problem on the bus trip because there's so much to talk about—like the school you went to, the family you left behind, and whether or not this is your first summer at camp. But just in case you need some good opening lines, feel free to memorize the following:

1. Do you always eat pickles on your peanut butter sandwiches?
2. Would you like a mint? You look a little green, and it really helps if you're feeling bus sick.
3. That's a great looking T-shirt. Did you make it?
4. I see you like_____, [Fill in appropriate rock group] I blew out my eardrum at their last concert.

GET SET

FIRST-DAY FACTS
AND FEARS

The first day of camp is only twenty-four hours long. Here's the break down: 2 hours to get your gear off the bus and into your cabin; 2 hours to unpack and meet the counselors and kids; 1 hour to find your way from the cabin to the Mess Hall; 1 hour to listen to Uncle Jay's "Welcome to this great camp" speech; 3 hours eating lunch and dinner; and finally 10 hours sleeping. That leaves only 5 hours to feel awkward, embarrassed, shy and scared!

Once you realize that the hard part is only five hours long, it will be easier to get through the first day. Everyone has doubts about adjusting to camp, so here are some common fears and facts to help you face the first day with a smile:

1. *Fear:* No one will like me at camp. I won't have any friends.

Fact: Worrying about making new friends at camp is natural, but meeting different kids is part of the adventure. Even if you traveled to camp with a friend from home, you'll find yourself making new friends during the summer.

2. *Fear:* I'll get the worst counselor at camp.

Fact: There's no such thing as the *worst* counselor—the ugliest counselor, maybe, or the tallest, fattest, thinnest, weirdest, dumbest, silliest, or sexiest—but not the worst. Counselors are really slightly bigger kids who came to camp for the same reason you did—to have a good time. They didn't come for the money! If you're basically a nice person (as opposed to an obnoxious jerk) your counselor will appreciate having you in his or her bunk. (For more tips on camper-counselor relationships, see "How to Handle Your Counselor," p. 43.)

3. *Fear:* I will be sick to my stomach, cry, or do something embarrassing like fart in the bunk.

Fact: Lots of people feel queasy when they get nervous. Try not to overload your stomach on the first day, and drink soda if you're feeling nauseated. (Belching is always permissible at camp.)

Crying is nothing to be ashamed of, but if you'd rather cry in private, try doing it in the shower (no one can hear you with all that water running). Or have a joke-telling session and hope to laugh hard enough to give you a reason to cry.

As far as farting goes, never say "Excuse me." Say, "Who did that?" and make a disgusted face.

CHOOSING YOUR BUNK BED

Probably the most important decision upon entering your cabin is whether you want the top or the bottom bed. Certain considerations should be made before choosing a bed. Top bunks are good if you want privacy, but they are the worst beds to have if a bat should fly into your bunk. Seeing a bat fly at eye level is a chilling experience. *Bottom bunks* are better for social kids who like other kids using their bed as a couch. Also, lower bunks are a must for sleepwalkers. If you want to stay friends with your bunk-bed partner, don't make bathroom visits in the middle of the night, and try not to toss and turn too much in your sleep.

When you enter your cabin and spot the bed of your dreams, throw your duffle bag on the bunk of your choice to claim it as your territory. Whatever bed you sleep in, remember to give the kids and counselors a fair chance. They'll all look better in the morning!

MEETING YOUR COUNSELOR

There are lots of ways to meet your counselor. Usually you are approached by one or two people wearing sun visors and carrying a clipboard who will claim to be your counselors. Now is the time to make a good impression. Smile, shake hands firmly, and state your name. This is also a good time for a brief biography of your likes and dislikes ("I like to keep my bunk neat, but I hate to get up in the morning!")

HOW TO HANDLE
YOUR COUNSELOR

A happy counselor can make your life a lot easier at camp. It may take some effort on your part to establish a good camper-counselor relationship, but the rewards are worth it! How else are you going to hear the best gossip in camp, get to borrow a great-looking T-shirt, or be saved from cleaning out the horse stalls after dinner? Counselors can really come in handy once you know how to handle them.

It's easy to get along with your counselors if you remember one simple fact: *Counselors are people, too.* They have good days and bad days, good moods and bad moods—they even have summer romances!

It's fun to watch for telltale signs of a Counselor In Love. Does your counselor daydream, sigh, stare at the stars, and lose track of time a lot? Is your counselor spending more time than usual in the shower, blow-drying his or her hair, or picking out clothes to wear to the campfire? Has your counselor lost his or her appetite to the danger point of *giving away* his last candy bar? If the answer is YES to one or more of these questions, your counselor is probably involved in a summer romance. (See "Counselor in Love/Camper in Love", p. 112.)

The point is that counselors experience a lot of the same ups and downs that *you* experience every day as a camper. If a counselor's love life is going well, he or she is going to be in a supergreat mood. If a counselor gets praise from the camp director for having the best-behaved bunk, he or she will glow with pride.

But counselors have bad days, too. *They* don't like playing baseball in 90-degree heat any more than *you* do. They too get grouchy being fed mystery meatloaf twice a week. Sometimes they feel homesick and lonely, and they love it when someone is cheerful and friendly and considerate of their feelings!

So how do you handle a counselor? The same way *you* want to be treated—with honesty, friendship, respect for his or her privacy, and patience for his or her moods. Sure, you've got to take care of your counselor once in a while! Do you think it's *easy* being responsible for a bunkful or screaming, fun-loving, sometimes-scared-of-the-water, always-full-of-poison-ivy, never-want-to-go-to-bed-or-get-up-in-the-morning kids?

So give your counselor a break now and then. When the going gets rough, get up early enough to be on time for flagpole lineup, change for swim without making a fuss, and just this once, skip the bread-ball fights at dinner.

CABIN LIFE

It's easy to adjust to life in a cabin, bunk or tent if you come from a large, noisy family who live in the woods without any TV's, telephones, stereos, video games, or other basic necessities of life.

If this sounds like *your* family, you'll feel right at home in a camp cabin! If, however, you come from a more conventional home with carpets on the floors and indoor plumbing, then you may take a little time getting used to your new environment. Cabin life is *not* a pampered, soft existence. It's rustic, back-to-nature stuff designed to make a *real man* or *woman* out of the softest camper.

Getting used to cabin life is usually a two-step process. First there's the *physical adjustment* to your strange new surroundings, and then there's the *emotional adjustment* to life in close quarters with lots of new kids who may also be strange. Add a counselor

who snores and picks her feet, and you're in for a few
more laughs and surprises.

Step One: PHYSICAL ADJUSTMENT

Most cabins, bunks or tents share a major feature—
rows of bunk beds with army surplus mattresses. Small
scraps of cloth hung on curtain rods cover the windows.

You may feel a little depressed at the sight of your
empty new home, but as soon as everyone moves their
junk in—including posters, quilts, pillows, stuffed an-
imals, mirrors, radios, alarm clocks, guitars, and sou-
venirs from home—it is suddenly transformed into a
very colorful dorm room. It's all casual and mixed up
and more fun than an overnight at your best friend's
house.

Step Two: EMOTIONAL ADJUSTMENT

It's always lots of laughs sharing a bedroom with six
or seven other kids—once you get used to it. Privacy
is a precious commodity at camp, so if you're a private
person, you may need a few days to get used to changing
your clothes in front of a roomful of people.

On the positive side, it's hard to be lonely with so
many kids to choose from for new friends. Keep an open
mind while getting to know your bunkmates. A shy
kid may seem "stuck up," and a noisy, outgoing kid
may hide his nerves behind a "cool" exterior. It's not
unusual for new campers to act differently from how
they normally act. They, too, have to adjust to camp.
But once the fun starts and everyone feels comfortable,
you'll get to see how everybody truly behaves. So, try
to be friendly and give everyone a chance.

CABIN CLEAN-UP

Most camps have certain rules about keeping cabins reasonably clean. Therefore you will probably be expected to perform the following chores as part of cabin clean-up:

1. Make your bed.
2. Pick up your clothes from the floor and under your mattress.
3. Eat your food *outside* (to keep the bugs outside).
4. Sweep the floor (if you have one).
5. Hang your wet towels and bathing suits on the line outside to dry. Wet clothes inside a cabin grow fungus, mildew, spores, and other green, fuzzy, moldy things.

Every day, before or after breakfast, your cabin will be inspected by an unbiased member of another cabin. Because of the competition to win cleanest-cabin-of-the-week award this person will judge your cabin harshly. A small, inconspicuous dust ball in the far left corner of your cabin could cost you one demerit. To end this degrading experience quickly—it pays to keep your cabin clean.

COMPETITION BETWEEN CABINS

Once you've settled into your cabin and made friends, you'll find that your cabin is a great source of unity, identity and pride. There's always some friendly competition between cabins as they try for camp awards like Cleanest Cabin, Cabin with the Most Camp Spirit, or Cabin with the Cutest Counselors. You'll want your cabin to be the *best* one in camp at all times.

Raids by other cabins are sometimes conducted in

the spirit of intercabin camp fun. Underwear is the most popular item to "borrow" from another cabin. Sometimes cabins have "mix-up days" so they can borrow different counselors or kids for fun and pranks. Imagination is the key to intercabin competition—but remember to return the counselor with his own underwear before the end of the summer.

RAINY DAYS

Soggy, mushy, full of mildew—that's a rainy day at camp.

But sometimes rainy days bring unexpected treasures—like a movie in the Rec Hall, or a trip to town to go bowling, eat pizza and play video games. Rainy days are good for all kinds of quiet activities, too—reading, exchanging camp gossip, playing cards or games, strumming on your guitar, and *writing letters*. (Remember those folks at home who paid for camp and are still hoping to receive word from you?) For creative suggestions, see "Letters Home", p. 77.

Even at camp, some rain must fall. But if you use your time wisely, you may enjoy the rainy days as much as the sunny ones. Here are some ideas for what to do on a rainy day:

1. Write in your diary.
2. Read the books Mom or Dad packed for you so

your brain won't turn to mush over the summer.

3. Get a head start on school. Write your composition now on "How I Spent My Summer Vacation."

4. Teach (or learn) a new card trick, new jokes, or a new song. Make up funny lyrics to songs you already know.

5. Turn out the lights and tell ghost stories.

6. Play jacks or Scrabble or Trivial Pursuit.

7. Hide your counselor's clothes (but remember where to find them).

HELP! THE LAUNDRY
ATE MY SHORTS

Most camps send clothes, sheets and blankets out of camp to be washed. This usually means your laundry travels by truck to the nearest town laundromat. If you're really in the wilderness, your laundry is shipped to the nearest area of civilization—possibly in another state. Either way one fact is clear: If your clothes *do* get returned to you, they will travel many miles before they are back in your cubby, washed, starched, shrunken, and full of holes.

But your clothes can survive a summer at camp if you take a few precautions to defeat the camp laundry system. Maybe you never do this at home, but if you have a special outfit or piece of clothing you cherish, *do not* send it to the camp laundry. Wash it yourself in the sink, or try wearing it into the shower, soap, rinse well, and hang it on a clothesline to dry. (Remember to remove yourself from the clothes first.)

Label everything, because camp laundries are strange creatures with peculiar eating habits—a favorite meal consists of three socks, two pairs of underwear, and the collar of your shirt. Strange outfits will appear in your laundry bag, while some of your own clothes are mysteriously missing. If your clothes are properly labeled, a kind camper may actually return them to you.

MESS HALL ETIQUETTE

Dining at camp is an experience you won't want to miss. The noise, the smells, the crashing of trays are all very exciting and part of mealtime entertainment.

Meals at camp are usually served *family style* (all the food is dumped in the middle of the table), or *cafeteria style* (you move down a line with a tray in your hands and try to catch the food as it's thrown to you).

SOME RULES OF ETIQUETTE:

1. When you lift the cover off a dish of food, do not yell "Gross out!" Some campers love franks 'n succotash. Wait till they serve *your* favorite which is someone else's gross-out!
2. Belching at camp falls into a special category. It is often excusable due to the meals served! However, spitting is absolutely not allowed.

3. Eating with fingers is allowed when handling chicken, corn on the cob, apples and bananas. It is unbecoming, however, when faced with chocolate pudding, Jell-O or mashed potatoes.

MEALTIME ANNOUNCEMENTS

Camp directors love to make announcements during meals, which is a signal for twenty or thirty campers to drop their trays on the floor or burst into song. Cheers, applause, whistles and boos are expected after major announcements, such as plans for a movie in town (cheers) or a big clean-up before Visiting Day (boos). Camp directors are trained to cope with these reactions, even though they turn red, get mad and blow their whistles for quiet.

FOOD FIGHTS

Food fights begin at camp when one inspired camper says, "This hamburger isn't fit to eat, but it sure makes a great hockey puck." Other kids follow, often with new ideas, like sliding Jell-O down someone's back, or giving someone a chocolate-pudding facial.

You can't plan a food fight—spontaneity is essential. If food fights are popular at your camp, but you find them disgusting, wear a raincoat to meals.

FOOD

Face it: You can't survive on Reese's Pieces all summer long. You've got to eat something served at camp. The trick is knowing what to eat and what to avoid like the plague. Camp food varies only slightly from camp to camp, so follow these guidelines:

1. Do *not* eat anything that crawls across the table. Chocolate-covered ants may be a delicacy in France, but at camp it means the cook forgot to hide the ant traps *behind* the stove.
2. Never eat blue food. Unless the food is blueberries or ices, blue food is either contaminated or part of a prank devised by the arts-and-crafts group.
3. Avoid mystery meat. Vegetables and fruits are safer and easier to identify. Anything round, hard and red is usually an apple. But something soft, mushy, and grayish-brown *could* be steak. Then again, it could be someone's missing baseball mitt.

4. Don't mess with furry food. Fur on food indicates mold, or fungus, or the camp director's dog. Furry food tickles the roof of your mouth and makes you cough up fur balls hours after eating.

5. Do not drink too much bug juice. You think it tastes good as it's going down, but the ultrahigh levels of sugar will have you flitting around camp like a deranged gnat. Why do you think they call it *bug* juice?

6. Pass up the "Chef's Special." The only thing special about this dish is the creativity of the chef. Who else can take three-day-old hamburgers and mixed vegetables, throw them together and turn out a "delectable" goulash?

7. Don't be fooled by Hawaiian Night. Just for fun, camps like to transform certain dinners into special meals with clever themes—Hawaiian Night is always popular, featuring a real luau. Other themes might be Chinese Banquets, Texas Barbeques, or Italian Pasta Parties. But don't be surprised if the food tastes *exactly* the same as every other night. It *is* the same, except for the ridiculous costumes you or the waiters are supposed to wear!

If you're wondering what you *can* eat at the Mess Hall without messing up your insides, memorize this list of safe foods (every camp is sure to have most of them):

1. Packaged dry cereal.
2. Milk in cartons.
3. Raw fruit. Be sure to wash it first—by the time you get a plum, it's been handled twenty-two times.
4. Ice cream.

5. Ketchup.
6. Mustard.

THE NEED FOR JUNK FOOD

Most campers need junk food, but camps like to downplay this fact. The most obvious source of junk food at camp is the Canteen, a little "store" that was invented by the camp directors and seems like a department store of goodies to you while at camp. Even so, if you feel the need for more goodies, consider requesting junk food from those you love.

CARE PACKAGES

MOM, DAD OR OTHER PARENT FIGURE

No one in your family has baked since the discovery of frozen cupcakes, but that doesn't matter now. One word from you and cakes, cookies and brownies will travel the airways and postal routes across America. Sometimes sending a short but direct letter helps.

Dear Mom [or Dad or name used for Step-Mom or Dad],
I know you're spending money to send me here, but please send your special chocolate fudge cake. It reminds me of home, and I miss you.
Love,
Your son/daughter [Name]

58

GRANDMA

The Grandma who fed you your first solid food when Mom wasn't looking—a nice cheese Danish—is the ultimate source of junk food. Grandma knows best when it comes to feeding you, so don't forget to write to her:

> *Dear Grandma,*
> *The food here is awful. I've lost five pounds in two days (don't tell my Mother). Please send one of your great apple pies, my favorite coconut cake, and a pound of rocky road fudge. I'm too weak to write anymore.*
> *Love,*
> *Your Devoted grandson/granddaughter [Name]*

BEWARE OF SABOTAGE!

Did your parents get a letter something like this one before you went to camp?

> *Dear Parents:*
> *We discourage care packages at camp. Please do not send junk food in the mail. These packages will be confiscated!*
>
> > *Sincerely,*
> > *Uncle Jay and Aunt Lucy*

You're exercising and working off millions of calories at camp. You deserve a treat. To conduct reverse sabotage and collect the rewards of a junk food binge, simply read these instructions:

1. Small boxes of candy can be hidden inside letters mailed in 3"×5" manila envelopes. It helps if Mom writes *Personal and Confidential* on the envelope.

2. Bigger junk food like tins of cookies or cakes have historically made their way carefully packaged for maximum camouflage!

> Pack food between layers of sweaters or pants. Have Mom mark the package *Warm Clothes for Junior.*

> Hide Candy in musical instrument cases. Write *Fragile: Musical Instrument* on the box.

> Send candy in bottles, which look like medication but aren't. Write on the package: *Urgent! Bunny's Growth Pills Inside!*

SPORTS

Whether or not you're at Sports Camp, you'll find all kinds of ball sports are popular—baseball, football, soccer, volleyball, tether ball, tennis, Ping-Pong and even jacks. You may want to try something new like fencing, horseback riding, archery or gymnastics. Even hopelessly uncoordinated kids can choose form a multitude of less strenuous sports like marbles, bingo, poker or pie eating.

To add to the sports excitement, some camps hire professional athletes to coach sports. This could be your big chance to find out if you've got what it takes to become someone who may win an Olympic medal or go on to a great career selling running shoes or deodorant on TV!

Whatever sport you choose, you have to learn how to handle the competition that goes along with the games at camp. A little healthy competition can help you run faster or throw farther, but it can also give you a stomachache. Don't forget: Winning isn't *everything*, and some crowds always love the underdog!

There's always competition at camp—between kids or between cabins. Try to behave in a sportsmanlike manner:

1. When choosing teams, don't always pick the most athletic kids first. If you choose a kid who is near-sighted, uncoordinated, and can't find first base without a map, you don't necessarily have to lose. Just pick the best player next. (This is good for confusing the opposing team, too!)
2. Special note for boys: If you are forced to play coed sports, *don't* say to a girl: "You play like a *girl!*"
3. Special note for girls: If you are forced to play coed sports, *don't* say to a boy: "You play like a *girl!*"
4. Winning and Losing
   a) Be a humble winner. It's great to win, but ob-noxious to act as if it was *easy*. Congratulate the other team (or player) for putting up such a good fight. (You might be on the losing side next time).
   b) Learn to lose graciously. Throwing athletic equipment around and stamping your feet on the ground is not the best way to behave when you lose (even though some professional ath-letes behave this way). Serious cursing should be reserved for the privacy of your cabin or the shower. (Remember, you might be on the win-ning side next time.)

Dear Doug,
   We just came back from an overnight that was great. First we hiked up a mountain, then we pitched ou

tents and took our blow-up raft out on the lake. There were only five of us and one counselor on this outing. It was sort of like a survival test. We had to do all our own fishing. And we even went hunting for berries!

I'm glad you're getting the arm back in shape. We'll need it this September. Mark writes me a lot. He says it's boring back home without us there. I told him to come up with my folks on visiting day and to bring me some junk food. You should drop him a letter and get him psyched up for the great baseball team we're going to have this fall.

Mitch

P.S.—I'm getting tired of fish and baked potatoes, so if you have any to spare, please send junk food for a needy, loyal friend.

Dear Mitch,

Well, we creamed the Royal Chargers, 6–0. When the bus pulled out of the camp, we all lowered our windows and shouted "Goodbye Royal Flops!" Some of the guys on their team got really pissed off and threw their caps at the bus. The camp director stopped the bus and made us apologize. So we all said we were sorry, and when the bus started up again, three of the guys in the backseat mooned! I never laughed so hard in my life.

Overall, camp is great but the food here is worse than the food at home. I bet you can't believe that! I wrote my grandmother a letter telling her I was going to be the first great baseball player to weigh under 100 lbs. Two days later I got this big brown box in the mail. When I opened it I thought I was dreaming. Get this: 6 packs of gum, black and red licorice, 10 chocolate bars, peanuts, crackers with cheese inside, homemade oatmeal cookies, and a pair of socks! You know how the camp laundry is!

I'm sending you a mini junk food package, after all "share and share alike."

> The best buddy you'll
> ever have,
> Doug

SWIMMING

Swimming is a Very Important sport at camp, because so many camps boast about a beautiful lake (better known as "the mud hole"), or about their Olympic-sized swimming pool. City kids are expected to learn how to swim at camp, and suburban kids are expected to return to school able to lead the swim team to glory and state championships.

Camp swimming really is a lot of fun—even if the air is full of mosquitoes and the lake is full of tadpoles. For one thing, you get to show off your new bathing suit. Next, you get to cool off. And last—if your timing is good—you get to watch your favorite fully clothed counselor pushed into the lake.

Here are a few tips to further your enjoyment of camp swims:

1. Don't go in the water without a bathing suit—unless you don't mind being kept out of the evening social.

2. Don't go in the water after eating camp food. You're going to leave a greasy ring around the lake.
3. Don't go in the water without a bathing cap. Getting the mud out of your hair will require a full bottle of creme rinse.
4. Don't go in the water without a buddy who's *really* a buddy!

FIELD TRIPS

Just when you thought it was safe to go out in a canoe again, here comes another field trip! Whether paddling across the lake with the midday sun in your eyes, or hiking through miles of woods with a five-pound pack on your back, field trips are a mixture of pleasure and pain that is synonymous with camp life!

The pain comes first—sore feet, aching backs, poison ivy and enough insect bites to keep you hopping and scratching all night—but the unexpected pleasures usually make the trip worthwhile. "Camping Out" takes on new meaning when you watch the sun set over the lake at dusk, cook hot dogs, hamburgers and S'Mores over an open fire, and stay up past midnight telling ghost stories and listening for strange footsteps in the woods. (You never know when Big Foot will decide to visit!)

Of course, field trips can also mean big-city treats—

a trip into town to see a movie, or a ride to the local bowling alley on a rainy day, followed by a genuine junk-food high at an ice-cream shop. Part of the fun of "going into town" is catching the local scenery of the very rural towns where many camps are located. Sometimes town is little more than one combination general store/gas station/restaurant.

Artsy-craftsy camps, or camps near college towns or larger cities, like to provide high-class cultural field trips to see plays, attend ballet performances, or soak up the sounds of classical music from a symphony orchestra. Be sure to bring a pillow for the bus trip back to camp—culture can be very tiring!

HOMESICKNESS

There are two essential facts to remember about homesickness: *Everyone* has it, and it will go away. Sometimes it goes away quickly, and sometimes it takes a little longer. Often it reappears in the middle of camp (after a phone call from home, or after seeing your parents on Visiting Day).

Just what is homesickness anyway? Dictionaries define it as an illness of the heart caused by missing home. You miss your home when you're away because you forget how often your parents nag you to clean up your room, take out the garbage, walk the dog and finish your homework. It's amazing what you can forget when you're so many miles away!

The best thing to do when you're homesick is to talk about it. Since every kid in camp is going to be homesick at one time or another, you'll have lots of company. Instead of hiding your feelings, you can share them and help other kids feel better, too. Or you can gather around in a circle and talk about the different things you especially like about camp. Like when your group hid all the oars to the canoes so the girl counselors couldn't paddle out to the boy counselors' beaches. Before you know it, everyone will be laughing and thinking about camp instead of home. (See "Brother/Sister at Camp.")

BROTHER/SISTER AT CAMP

Having a brother or sister at camp is what's known as a mixed blessing. While it's nice to see a familiar face in the Mess Hall, you don't want your little sister or brother trailing after you all day long. And what if this person who is your relative acts like a jerk? This reflects badly on *you* since you share the same family name. Even worse, what if your blood relative excels in sports or gets the lead in the camp play, while you sit on the sidelines feeling inferior?

One of the biggest problems regarding brothers and sisters at camp is competition. Worrying about which one of you is going to be the "better' or "more popular" camper can ruin your summer vacation!

The only way to resolve this competition is to end it, once and for all, at camp. Think of how *mature* you will feel when you sit down together and conclude that it's unimportant to try and outdo each other. Discuss

71

the fact that you are *two separate individuals* with very separate identities and individual strengths and weaknesses. This could be the beginning of a whole new relationship for the two (or three or four) of you! In fact, sometimes when you're homesick, the best thing to do is to visit your brother or sister. A few choice words and you'll forget about the blue feelings you have.

If, however, your superstar sister or brother refuses to give up the challenge, then take a solemn vow *never* to reveal the true nature of your family ties. After all, lots of people have the same last name!

BROTHERS/SISTERS AT DIFFERENT CAMPS

Some parents send their children to different camps, even if it means traveling four hundred miles on Visiting Day. They think that by separating their kids they will avoid sibling rivalry. But they overlooked one major area of competition: Whose camp is better? For brothers and sisters, this information can easily be obtained through carefully worded letters.

Here's a sample letter to get you on your way:

Dear_____[Fill in appropriate name],

So how's it going at camp? Life at Camp Anoola is great! Last night was The Big Beef Barbeque—we had steak, hamburgers, roast beef, corn on the cob, watermelon, chocolate cake and two kinds of ice cream. Everything tasted so good, I ate until I almost split my jeans. What did you have for dinner last night?

After dinner we saw a double-feature horror movie (the kind Mom and Dad never let us watch at home). That's what I love about this camp. They're very progressive here.

Tomorrow is Backwards Day, so we get to sleep late and eat dessert before every meal. We're always doing something special at Camp Anoola. What kind of special activities do you have?

It's too bad you didn't decide to come here, but I'm sure your camp has one or two fun things to do.

Love,

[Your Name]

P.S. I would miss you a lot, but I'm having too much fun.

GO FOR IT!

LETTERS HOME

No matter how anxious your parents are to get you on the bus to camp, the minute you leave they turn into sentimental slobs. They cry and carry on about what a great kid you are, and how quiet and empty the house seems without you. Parents are like that.

You wouldn't want your parents to worry about you—not *too* much, anyway. Maybe just enough to get your bedtime pushed back an hour. That's why letters home are so important. You want your parents to keep on missing you (so they'll *really* be glad to see you when you get home!).

While you're on the bus, write your first letter home. Feel free to copy this one exactly:

Dear Mom and Dad,
    I know we just said goodbye, but I miss you already. I wasn't sure I wanted to go to camp this

summer, but I wanted to make you happy. I guess it will be great for you two to be alone together for the first time in——years [fill in your age].

I'll try to have a good time, but it won't be easy. Please don't worry about me. I have your picture in my wallet, and I think I'll put it under my pillow when I get to camp. I MISS YOU.

> *Love and Kisses,*
> *[Your Name]*

Put a few drops of water on the letter and smudge the ink to make it look like you've been crying. Mail the letter as soon as you get to camp, so your parents will get it right away. Your Mom will want to race right up to camp and bring you home, but your Dad will talk her out of it. "I've got a better idea," he'll say. "Let's send our darling some of your famous oatmeal-raisin cookies and a picture of his hamster."

After all, it isn't easy being away from home.

Don't try to get away with just one letter. Here's an all-purpose form letter that's easy to use on a weekly basis. Just fill in the blanks from this handy list of suggestions, and mail. Results are guaranteed:

Dear Mom and Dad,

Hi! How are you? I'm okay, I guess. Yesterday I had to see the camp nurse because I had an attack of [a]. Don't worry. She said it probably won't leave any scars.

I passed my [b] swimming test! Now I can swim alone at night in the lake! That should be lots of fun.

The food here is [c]. You better send my vitamin pills fast. We never get any real [d]. Just fake stuff loaded with preservatives. It's a good thing I can buy all the [e] I want at the Canteen or I might starve to death.

I miss you [f]. Please kiss my little [g]. I miss [him, her, it] a lot, too. Please write soon. I live for your letters but don't worry about me.

Love and Kisses,
[Your Name]

SUGGESTIONS FOR BLANKS

(a)	(b)	(c)
poison ivy	tadpole	gross
trench mouth	porpoise	awful
worms	dolphin	disgusting
appendicitis		inedible

(d)	(e)	(f)
milk	candy	a lot
juice	soda	terribly
meat	gum	with all my heart
vegetables	popcorn	every minute of the day

(g)
sister
brother
hamster
dog

K.P.

K.P. is an army abbreviation meaning Kitchen Patrol. In the army it usually means peeling potatoes and scrubbing pots. Since camp is supposed to be more fun than the army, duties are more creative—like putting maraschino cherries on top of 412 servings of tapioca pudding, or husking twenty bushels of corn.

Not all camps assign K.P., but for those that do, most campers believe it's because the camp directors think K.P. builds character twelve ways.

Here's what you can expect in the line of K.P. duty:

1. Food Preparation
    Chores include potato peeling, string-bean snapping, turnip squashing, corn husking, and smashing lumps in the oatmeal.
2. Dishing Out Slop
    As campers move down the cafeteria line, you get

to exercise your pitching arm by tossing the food onto the moving trays. If your arm is bad, this is a great way to start a food fight. For some kids, the steam tables are a great way to clear up a problem complexion!

3. Bussing Tables
   Want to get a member of the opposite sex to really sit up and notice you? Try pouring ice water into his or her lap!

4. Clean Up
   If you're not squeamish, or if you have the appetite of an elephant with an iron stomach, this is a great way to cash in on juicy leftovers. Or consider turning a stash of dried up peas into a lovely necklace for Mom.

HOW TO AVOID K.P.

K.P. is probably the easiest camp chore to avoid, because the Board of Health has certain rules regarding food and dishes. Get yourself a case of any of the following and you're K.P.-free for the summer:

1. Poison ivy or sumac
2. Eczema
3. Impetigo
4. Cold sores
5. Trench mouth
6. Worms
7. Any open wound

GROSS-OUTS AND DISEASES

The following activities, events and things are definitely considered gross at camp:

kissing with Hubba Bubba gum in your mouth
greasy hair
leeches, lice and liver
trench mouth
black socks
throwing up in the cabin
poison ivy below the waist
picking pimples in public
cutting your toenails outside the Mess Hall
food fights (fun, but still gross)
mashed potatoes in your hair (caused by the above)
wet bathing suits in bed
the camp director in his underwear

FUNGUS

A fungus is the kind of growth you would rather do without. Unfortunately, it grows very well at camp because of all the dark, moist places there. Fungi do not like sunshine and fresh air.

Athlete's foot is a kind of fungus that grows between your toes. (Dark and moist there, right?) Of course if you have webbed feet you don't have to worry about athlete's foot.

Fungus can be fun as long as it stays off your body. Bunk fungus (otherwise known as "Creeping Rot") can be colorful and picturesque. Just try leaving a wet bathing suit between the sheets or under your sleeping bag. (They'll probably invite a scientist to collect samples and rare specimens of your fungus for future research projects.)

NURSE
(AND OTHER ILLNESSES)

Camp nurses usually come in two varieties: sweet, kind mothering types and old battle-axes who nursed their way through the Civil War. The Infirmary houses the best beds in camp—the ones with *real* mattresses and *real* sheets. Some infirmaries are even equipped with *television*. Although its better to be out on the playing field, a sick camper can survive being in the infirmary. here's a sample of what you can expect:

MALADY	TREATMENT
Trench mouth. A camp specialty, these sores on the mouth are caused by dirty dishes and silverware	Gentian violet (known as the "Purple Curse") will be painted all over your mouth. This may evoke interesting responses from members of the opposite sex.

Sprains, sore muscles, and other sports injuries	Ben Gay will be spread on your limbs, after which you will be wrapped in Ace bandages and given a pair of crutches—no matter which part of your body is actually injured. (Nurses know that injured campers are usually very dramatic.)
Bee, wasp and other stings	You get to take a real bath in the only camp bathtub, after which Nurse crushes ice cubes, puts them in a plastic bag, and applies it to the painful areas of your body.
Stomach aches	Nurse will attempt to engage you in a fascinating conversation about your bathroom habits. Tell her (or him) the last time you went was at Howard Johnson's on the way to camp, right after eating a marshmallow butterscotch sundae. You can avoid prunes or castor oil by describing to Nurse in vivid detail

what terrible things
happen if you are forced
to swallow these
disgusting substances.

The Runs

Also known as diarrhea,
the galloping trots, and
camp's revenge. Nurse
will recommend
Kaopectate (white
medicine that looks,
tastes, and smells like
chalk) or Pepto Bismol
(pink stuff that tastes like
bad bubblegum). You may
enjoy lying on a hot-
water bottle and sipping
ginger ale while you and
Nurse watch "All My
Children."

Poison ivy, oak and
sumac

Calamine lotion (the
"Pink Curse") will be
spread over your entire
body. You will then be
wrapped in sterile gauze,
which you can treat as a
cast and have fellow
campers sign.

Dear Doug,
  I bet you wouldn't recognize me if I stood right in
your face! I look like some sort of pink Martian from
outer space. On our last campfire I went looking for

kindling to keep the flames going. It was dark and I couldn't find my flashlight. I must have stepped right smack into a patch of poison ivy. The nurse put this pink gook all over me—even in places that don't itch! Now I can't go swimming for a few days.

I've decided to take up guitar. My counselor, Jim, plays the guitar and he's really good. He said he'd teach me. I'm going to practice during swim, that way I won't get bored sitting on the dock. Maybe if I get good enough I can play along with Jim at the next campfire.

Hey, thanks a lot for the goods—they really hit the spot. You're a real pal.

Mitch

Dear Mitch,

Camp has taken a turn for the worse. Remember that social at the beginning of camp? Well, I never told you what happened that night. Our camp went over to this girls' camp across the lake. There was a band playing in the rec hall for the older kids, while the younger kids played games in the mess hall. At the dance I met this really cute girl named Cindy. She has big blue eyes and giggles a lot. But boy is she a serious dancer. She could dance for hours—I couldn't keep up with her.

Every Friday we visit one another's camp to have our social. Last Friday I asked Cindy to take a walk with me. She's so cute and I never seem to get the chance to be alone with her. So we went for a walk behind the stables. Just when I was about to plant one on her this flashlight shines right in my face! It was

my counselor, and boy was he mad! Now I have K.P.
duty for a week! It's the penalty I have to pay for
leaving the rec hall. Seven nights of making gallons of
bug juice. I just hope I don't turn into another "pesty"
camper—HA HA!

Doug

BEST FRIENDS

What almost makes up for leaving your best friend at home this summer? Finding a bunch of new friends at camp.

Friendships are practically guaranteed when you live, swim, eat, shower, play and party with so many kids. It's hard *not* to make friends at camp.

Some kids like to jump right into a friendship with a bang, while others take their time. If you're a quiet, cautious person, it may be easier for you to make friends slowly, one at a time. You can start with a bunkmate and branch out from there. Look for friends at special activities that *you* enjoy, whether boxing or ballet, swimming or softball. Common interests are always a good basis for friendship. And don't ever be afraid to make the first move. Everyone likes to be noticed and appreciated, so walk right up to a kid and start talking.

If you're an outgoing kind of kid, you're used to making the first move, which is fine. Just remember not to overwhelm everyone with your natural enthusiasm. (It's always a good idea to let the other kid talk once in a while!)

Whatever your style, camp is a great place for exploring new opportunities, adventures and experiences, including friendships. So when you're down to your last chocolate-chip cookie, break it in half and go make a new friend.

Dear Jenny,

I guess it's pretty exciting to fall in love with an older man, but aren't there rules about things like that? To be perfectly honest, I'm glad my camp is divided into two separate camps, with the boys across the lake. I don't think I could deal with boys for breakfast, lunch and dinner. It's bad enough we're going to have our first social this Saturday night, which makes me a nervous wreck. It's easy for you, you were born boy crazy, but I never know what to say. What if nobody asks me to dance? Should I volunteer to serve refreshments that night? At least that way I'll look busy if the whole thing turns out to be a social disaster.

I decided to give sports a fair trial as long as I'm here. So far, I've tried tennis, softball, swimming, volleyball, fencing and jogging (I can't believe people do that for fun). I haven't found a sport I like yet, but guess what? I sweated off four pounds!!!

I guess things are getting better, because I'm only homesick about once a week now. Tryouts for the big play on Visiting Day are being held tomorrow, and I really want a part, so keep your fingers crossed for me. Wouldn't it be great if we could visit each other on

Visiting Day! I can't believe two weeks of camp are over already. Time sure flies when you're out of school!

Love,
Betsy

Dear Betsy,

I hope you get a great part in the play.

You won't believe what happened to me this morning—I twisted my ankle sliding for second base! I'm writing this letter to you from the camp infirmary, where I'm resting with an ice pack on my swollen foot. (It's not broken. They x-rayed it in the hospital in town.) The only good thing about being here is that there's a real live TV!!! You remember TV—that box with sound and moving people! It sure is great to catch up on my favorite soap operas. I don't even mind watching old reruns.

All I can say is, this foot better be in shape before Color War! Do you have Color War at your camp? You must. Some camps don't, because they think it's too competitive, which is insane! For me, the competition is almost the best part.

I wonder what Greg will do when he sees that I'm wounded?! Do you think sympathy is good for a romance? Speaking of romance, how was your camp social? Let me know if you met anyone interesting.

Love from your wounded pal,
Jennifer.

P.S.—Please send junk food!!! My supply has run out, and I'm having a candy attack! Would you believe this canteen only sells health food snacks like granola bars (yuk!). Can you get real candy at Na-Sha-Pa? Please mail it to me in a plain brown envelope. Write: For the sick and wounded. Thanks—you may save my life!

THE CAMP SOCIAL

One of the most eagerly anticipated events at camp (especially if your camp is all girls or all boys) is the Camp Social. Next to a romantic campfire, this is the best way to get to know a member of the opposite sex on a more personal level. Here's your chance to wear clean clothes, listen to music, dance and flirt. (For pointers, please see "Flirting in Field and Stream," p. 107 and "Kissing," p. 110.)

Camp socials can have lots of different themes and activities, depending on your camp's creativity and the supplies in the Arts and Crafts Shop. Themes can range from "The Dating Game" to "Punk Night at Camp Cayuga." Most often a Camp Social includes dancing of some kind, but it may be something corny and campy like folk dancing or square dancing.

Camp socials are definitely casual affairs, so there's no reason to get nervous about them. If you've picked up a boyfriend or girlfriend at camp, then it's definitely fun to go as a couple. But most kids go to socials in large groups of friends and bunkmates.

Just in case you feel shy at your first Camp Social, here are some clever ideas to help break the ice:

1. Spend a lot of time around the refreshment area. This is the most popular spot to hang out at a Camp Social, and a great place to meet different kids who stop by for some bug juice and cookies.

2. Dance with a friend—any friend. If you're out on the dance floor, you'll look and feel like you're part of the action. It's sometimes easier while dancing to talk to other kids who are dancing near by.

3. Wear something *outrageous* (like a party dress and high heels if you're a girl; grungy cut-off jeans with a shirt, tie and jacket if you're a boy; or a punk outfit with green, spray-dyed hair (either sex). This is a great conversation starter, and a sure way to get noticed!

MUSIC

There's always music in the air at camp, from the first wake-up gong to the last strums on the guitars at night. In between there's rock blaring from radios in every bunk, orchestra rehearsals on the porch, chorus by the flagpole, and recorder lessons behind the barn.

If you play an instrument, by all means bring it to camp (unless it's the piano). Anyone can play in the camp orchestra as long as he knows how to get his instrument out of its case, and can make any kind of sound with it. If you've never played an instrument, here's your golden opportunity for private lessons. The music counselor is so lonely he will practically pay you to learn how to play the oboe. (Not too many kids come to camp specifically to play musical instruments.) Two noteworthy exceptions are the recorder and the guitar, which everyone wants to learn how to play at camp (especially if the folksinging counselors are cute). *Cho-*

rus is a popular musical activity, because all you need is your throat. Some camps include counselors in the chorus, which adds greatly to the enthusiasm of campers for this activity. (See " Counselor in Love / Camper in Love," p. 112.)

But the music that really means camp is *folk music*, involving guitars and songs that date back before rock, soul, reggae and breakdancing. No one is really sure how the music called *folksinging* became so closely associated with summer camp. Some say it happened when the very first camp director at the very first camp heard the very first campers singing around the very first campfire and said: "I sure love the sound of all those little folks singing!"

Folksinging is fun because you get to clap your hands, stamp your feet and sing along. No one cares if you can carry a tune, and the words are so repetitious anyone can learn them. Here's a typical African folk song sung at camp:

Kumbaya

Chorus: Kumbaya, my lord, Kumbaya
            Kumbaya, my lord, Kumbaya
            Kumbaya, my lord, Kumbaya
            Oh lord, Kumbaya.

Verse: Someone's_____my lord, Kumbaya
            Someone's_____my lord, Kumbaya
            Someone's_____my lord, Kumbaya
            Oh lord, Kumbaya.

Fill in the blanks with action verbs like "sleeping," "eating," et cetera.

COLOR WAR

The ancient tradition of Color War began in 1949 at Camp Thunderclap when Puny Pinky Brown challenged Whitey Whitman to an arm-wrestling contest. At 5 foot 11 inches tall and 200 pounds, Whitey was the odds-on favorite. Still, Pinky was a popular underdog, tipping the scales at a mere 93 pounds.

Weeks before the big challenge, Camp Thunderclap became divided into two opposing camps: Whitey's Team versus Pinky's Team. Soon the two teams worked themselves into a fevered pitch over this event. Whitey's Team began dressing only in white. They made up banners and songs and cheers to spur their hero on to victory. Not to be outdone, Pinky's Team dyed a bunch of T-shirts pink and coined the slogan: Pink is puny, but it's proud!

And so the tradition of Color War was born, though never understood. Now each summer camp stages a sort of Civil War by dividing the camp into two teams which then fight against each other. No one remembers how the first Color War games started but no one cares anyway.

BREAKOUT OR FAKEOUT

Everyone loves Color War, and around the middle of the season campers get anxious. Anything new or different at camp is suspected of being part of the Breakout scheme. But Breakout isn't always what it appears to be. Just imagine. You are sitting in the rec hall. The entire camp is here. The movie has ended, and the lights are switched on. Suddenly, there is a downpour of confetti. The crowd goes wild. Campers from every division are shouting and cheering. The music is turned on. Over the P.A. you hear the blare of a marching song. What else can it be but Breakout? Sure enough, you can see the banners waving in the distance. Your heart pounds as they get closer. You start to wonder if you'll be on the same team as Billy Martin, the best home-run hitter in all of Camp Anoola. You can barely control your excitement! The banners are now close enough to read. What are the teams called this summer—the Red Dragons and the Blue Bears? Those were the names of last year's teams! The truth settles in along with some disappointment. You know you have just been the victim of a Fakeout. But Fakeouts aren't all that bad, because you know that Color War is about to break any day.

When Color War Breakout finally happens, you'll know it's the real thing. Usually it occurs when you least expect it. You're taking a shower and you hear sirens. Over the loudspeaker Uncle Jay's voice booms "Everyone down to the lake!" You pull on your clothes, which stick to your wet body. Tripping over your shoe-laces you run down to the lake, where the rest of the camp is already assembled. There's word that Big Foot has been sighted roaming the shoreline. Police are everywhere. Uncle Jay is in a frenzy. Suddenly, a heli-copter appears. Men are shouting down to you through megaphones. A man in a blue uniform reaches into a bag. He's throwing down leaflets. You grab for one and run off into a clearing to read it. No, it can't be—it is, it's Color War Breakout and you're holding the team sheet! You are a member of the Blue Marlins along with the one and only Billy Martin!

The only event that is more exciting than Color War Breakout is the announcement of the winning team!

BLUE AND RED

Once the teams have been chosen and Color War is official, the atmosphere at camp changes. The gigantic family once known as Camp Anoola no longer exists. Now there are only two armies, and you are a member of either the Red or the Blue. Everything on the camp grounds is divided into Red and Blue. Even your cabin will be split down the middle. Red people will have to sleep on the Red side, and Blue people on the Blue side. There is absolutely no mixing. This is serious business! Never trust a member of the opposing team—even if he or she is your counselor. Many spies have been known to disguise themselves as "friends," only to win your confidence and sabotage your team's secret plans. So remember, mum's the word! Remain loyal to your team by keeping defense strategies to yourself.

WINNING AND NOT WINNING

When it comes to Color War, the rules change. It's not how well you play the game, it's whether or not you *win*. Winning is *everything* in Color War (although no one is sure why). Prizes are rarely given out to members of the winning team. The prestige and glory of being the winner is supposed to be enough.

Since winning is everything, campers often use "special rules." Color War involves very special kinds of strategies which can range from the simple to the sublime, depending on the creativity of your team. Here are some popular techniques you may want to try:

1. The night before a big game, steal the pants from the opposing team. This is known as catching them with their pants down.
2. Before a race, remove the shoelaces from the sneakers of the best runners.
3. Act as a spy. Disguise yourself as a short counselor and infiltrate a secret meeting to learn the dirty low-down tricks of the other team.
4. Before an eating contest, lure the best eater on the opposing team to an ice-cream parlor and offer to pay for his food!

SONGS, CHEERS, AND OTHER (SOMETIMES) SILLY STUFF

Although competition is fierce during Color War, there are plenty of silly, yet memorable, moments to break the tension. Eating contests are among the amusing events as camp chubbies vie for the cherished Pig-out Award over platters of steaming wienies or truckloads of fruit pies.

But the best stuff are the songs and cheers invented

by each team to boost camp spirit. These dramatic song-fests are performed morning, noon and night during Color War, at the highest possible volume achieved by the human voice.

Typical of the brilliant words composed for Color War cheers is this cheer written by the Blue Team at Camp Anoola:

> Blue is tough
> Blue is proud
> And we're gonna shout it loud!
> Blue is great in every way
> Blue will *cream* the Red
> today!*

There's not much hope these songs will win a Grammy, but they keep team spirit high (while making the other team *sick*).

*Copyright 1984: Camp Anoola Blue Team

SPECIAL SITUATIONS

DROPPING OUT OF A SPECIAL ACTIVITY THAT COSTS EXTRA MONEY

Remember how you *begged* your parents to spend the extra big bucks for horseback-riding lessons this summer? Remember how you just couldn't *live* without learning how to gallop and jump over hurdles?

Well, it's been two weeks now, and the smell of the stables isn't getting any sweeter. No one warned you that along with taking riding lessons came the responsibility of "horse care"—which translates into *shoveling manure!* No matter how many showers you take, the smell lingers on. Your backside has never been so sore, and all you've done is *walk* the dumb horse!

What are you going to do? Maybe the expensive activity you pleaded for was waterskiing or canoeing or fencing. It seemed so glamorous before you tried it.

Now all you want is to forget you ever heard of the sport.

You have several options in this situation. You can develop a sudden allergy to hay, which makes it impossible to be around horses. You can declare a new psychological fear of fencing that makes it impossible for you to handle sharp swords (even if they're rubber). But you've still got to explain it to your parents, unless you want to forfeit an entire year's allowance to pay for your mistakes.

Dear Mom and Dad,

Hello from Camp Anoola! Everything here is just great. I passed my Swimming Test yesterday, and I'm now an Advanced Intermediate. I'm really working hard on my_____ [fill in with a favorite activity like swimming, boating, baseball, drama, etc.]. In fact, it's what I enjoy most here at camp.

I have a very minor problem which I'd like to discuss with you. I'd certainly like your opinion on what to do. Remember the_____ lessons I signed up for before camp? Well, they've really been a unique experience, but they interfere with my new goal to become the best_____ [swimmer, baseball player, actress, etc.]. My counselor says I should learn to focus my attention on one activity, so I can really do it well. I hope you agree. I want you to be proud of me when I win the Best———Award at the end of the summer.

That's why I was wondering if perhaps I could drop the special_____ lessons. I know if you write to the camp director, he'll give you almost all your money back.

Thanks for understanding. You're the greatest.
                              Love and kisses,
                              [Your Name]

GETTING KICKED OUT

Getting kicked out of camp is a special situation you definitely want to avoid. Everyone breaks a rule now and then, but getting kicked out is usually reserved for breaking important rules that are designed for your safety and well-being. That's why you should never hitchhike into town by yourself, or swim unsupervised at night, or drink anything more alcoholic than bug juice.

If you want to leave camp that badly, there's always a way out (see "Fourteen Excuses for Leaving Camp Early"). And if you're just feeling lonely and want some attention, try standing on your head next to the flagpole. It's more fun, and you might even set a camp record.

FOURTEEN EXCUSES
FOR LEAVING CAMP EARLY

1. I've got a new baby [brother; sister; puppy; gerbil].
2. My dog is on a hunger strike until I come home.
3. It's almost harvest time, and I have to go home to help in the fields.
4. The best department store in town is having a back-to-school sale for one week only.
5. My braces need an immediate adjustment.
6. The Jacksons Are Coming to Town!!!!
7. My Mom just got accepted for college, and I have to go home to teach her how to use the computer.
8. My Dad just got a new job, and I have to go home to teach him how to use the computer.
9. My older [sister; brother] just got engaged, and I've got to meet the turkey who agreed to spend the rest of [his; her] life with that jerk!
10. August 1 is my birthday, and every year on my birthday the entire family gathers in our backyard

to celebrate this joyous event. It's bad luck to break a family tradition.

11. There is fungus growing on every part of my body. I have to go home to sleep in a dry place.

12. I have to go home to support the family to send my parents to camp.

13. My canteen money just ran out.

14. My parents miss me too much (although they're too brave to admit it). I have to go home before they die of loneliness.

THE OPPOSITE SEX
Flirting in Field and Stream

Camp is the ideal place to practice the fine art of flirting. There are all these romantic, off-beat places to meet—the old oak tree at the edge of the woods, the mud hole at night, or behind the stables (step carefully). And there are great opportunities for intimate conversation—while waiting on line for canteen, or before evening activities begin.

But what if you're new to the game of flirting and don't know how or when to begin? Here are sure-fire pointers on what to say and do.

CONVERSATION VERSUS BODY LANGUAGE

There are two major ways to flirt: with words and with *actions*. Sophisticated flirting combines both.

Conversation is a good way to start. Eye contact is very important—you shouldn't tell a girl how pretty she is while studying her toes, or compliment a boy on a great game of soccer while staring at his broad, bronzed shoulders.

Here are some suggestions for great flirting conversation. Choose answers a, b or c to suit your particular mood, situation or personality.

1. I love your_____.
    a) hair
    b) hamstrings
    c) T-shirt

2. You know, you're the best_____in camp.
    a) swimmer
    b) dancer
    c) shortstop

3. Of all the girls I've ever met, you're the_____.
    a) prettiest
    b) smartest
    c) strongest

4. Of all the boys I've met, you're the_____.
    a) nicest
    b) tallest
    c) fastest

5. Spending time with you is fun because_____.
    a) you're a great conversationalist
    b) you know how to make me laugh
    c) you've got real camp spirit!

6. Would you like to_____?
    a) take a walk with me
    b) share my last stick of bubblegum
    c) raid my bunk tonight

7. When we get home, I'll never_____.
   a) forget you
   b) fail to phone you
   c) find you in the city. Could you take the train
      here? I'm not allowed out after dark.

Kissing

Kissing is the camp activity of choice for after-dark hours. No experience is necessary, and all you have to bring is a blanket and your lips.

Before you begin kissing, there are a couple of things you should do:

1. Make sure your partner is of the opposite sex. With unisex hairdos and clothing, it's easy to mistake a girl for a boy, and vice versa. This could lead to some embarrassing moments.

2. Set the mood with some tasteful conversation. "How do you like camp?" is a good opening line. "What's your favorite activity here?" "Who is your counselor?" "Would you like a candy bar?" Each can set a mood. Only then should you say: "Let's try some kissing."

3. Length of kisses. This is a delicate area because everyone likes to kiss for a different length of time.

It's usually a good idea to mix short kisses with long ones, just for variety. Here's a good rule of thumb: It's hard to hold your breath for more than two minutes, so if your partner stops breathing, it's time to come up for air.

Here are some more good tips on kissing:

1. Always remove your bite plate.
2. Do not attempt to kiss and chew gum at the same time.
3. Try to finish your breath mint *before* kissing, to minimize the risks of choking.

Counselor in Love/
Camper in Love

Someone is always in love at camp. Counselors fall for other counselors, campers get crushes on other campers, C.I.T.'s go crazy for J.C.'s, and even married counselors start holding hands with each other as if they were just dating.

But the hardest kind of love to fall into at camp is the forbidden kind that happens every summer—a case of a camper in love with a counselor. Maybe it's more like a crush or an extreme case of "like," but either way it's a ticklish situation.

It's not that you *planned* to do anything silly like lose your heart to a guy who's old enough to be your uncle. But one day you're sitting at the lake waiting for your swimming lesson, and suddenly you see him in a different light. He's so tall and sophisticated, funny and handsome, tan and well-built. And best of all, he's *old enough to know how to talk to a girl without acting like a complete jerk!* Who could resist a man like that?

He's really been nice to you, too, spending extra time helping you perfect your backstroke. And he *does* call you "Shrimp" and mess up your hair every time you see him—isn't teasing a great sign of affection? Okay, so he's twenty-one and you're thirteen. Your age won't make a bit of difference when you're twenty-one and he's twenty-nine—if you can wait that long!

In the meantime, what can you do about this terrible longing to be with him? You can, of course, take extra swimming lessons (or guitar, arts and crafts, tennis, riding—whatever he or she is in charge of) just to be near the object of your fantasies. You can practice your flirting techniques if you don't overdo it. Throwing yourself at the feet of your counselor is *definitely* not the right move. It's always possible that this counselor thinks you're adorable, but remember: The first rule for counselors at camp is No fooling around with the campers.

The best thing you can do is to take advantage of your crush. Try out your social skills for the future. Learn how to talk, joke, smile and walk, all at the same time—and without blushing! Enjoy a conversation with someone who can give you good advice on what appeals to an older man or woman. Get a head start on the most difficult dating maneuver—eating a meal with someone you like—by sitting next to your special counselor at a camp picnic or barbeque. If you can learn how to spit out watermelon pits next to the one you adore, you're well on your way to becoming a social success.

Think of your crush on a counselor as great practice in the art of love. And you know what they say about practice—in a few years, you'll be perfect.

The Love Quiz

Summer camp is the best place in the world to fall in love for the first time. There's something so romantic about singing songs before an open campfire, canoeing on the lake at sunset, or watching a movie and holding hands. Love is always in the air at camp.

But how can *you*, a newcomer to the game of love, know if it's The Real Thing? Maybe it's just indigestion from last night's pizza party.

The Love Quiz is designed to help you find out how seriously you've fallen in love. Check *one* answer in each category that best describes the way you feel. Each answer has a point score. At the end of the quiz, add up your points and find out if you've got a case of *real love*. (Also check "Counselor in Love/Camper in Love," p. 112.)

Category I: SOUNDS

a) You hear bells ringing and you're sure you never even packed your alarm clock. (4 points)

b) You wait for the phone to ring for you, even though there aren't any phones at camp. (3 points)

c) You think you hear sweet nothings being whispered in your ear. (2 points)

Category II: APPETITE

a) You're never hungry. (4 points)

b) You have cravings for rich chocolate. (3 points)

c) You're starving all the time—even camp food smells good! (2 points)

Category III: READING HABITS

a) You read a lot of poetry and even try writing some. (4 points)

b) You read *Seventeen* for tips of dating and teen romance. (3 points)

c) You read *True Confession Magazine* and try to borrow the counselor's romance novels. (2 points)

Category IV: LONGINGS AND DESIRES

a) You don't even miss anyone from home when you're at camp. (4 points)

b) You miss your pets. (3 points)

c) *For girls:* You miss bumping into the football coach in the hall. (2 points)

For boys: You miss seeing the captain of the cheerleading squad show off her red underwear when she does a leap. (2 points)

SCORING

Scoring is the same for girls and boys. Add up all your points.

If you scored 8–11 points—You have a crush on some-one or a case of indigestion. Both will clear up when the summer is over.

If you scored 12–15 points—You're involved in Puppy Love. This is a condition that prepares you for the real thing.

If you scored 16 points—Congratulations! You've got a case of *real love*, which may even last into September. Consult an older teen-ager, counselor or other expert, on how to proceed in the game of love.

VISITING DAY

Most camps prepare for Visiting Day the way the United States government prepares for World War III. There are secret meetings far into the night. Special events like camp plays and Olympic games are planned. Uncle Jay can be observed having a nervous breakdown as he desperately tries to transform the camp grounds, mud hole and counselors to match the wholesome images illustrated in the camp brochure.

Visiting Day is a very important event at camp. For you, it's the first time you've seen your parents in many weeks. For the camp directors, it's a chance to prove that camp was worth all the money your parents spent to send you there! This is why you'll have the best meal of the summer the night before V-Day, featuring *real meat*, lots of fresh vegetables and fruit, and apple pie or hot fudge sundaes for dessert. Any camp director worth his whistle knows that the first question out of

Mom's mouth when she sees you will be, "What did you have for dinner last night?"

But clearly the main event on Visiting Day is *showing off*—for you and the camp. Showing off is a lot easier if you are an only child or *the* only child from your family at camp. If you have sisters or brothers with you at camp, you're going to have to share the spotlight and Mom and Dad's attention with them. (See "Brother/Sister at Camp," p. 71.) Try to schedule and coordinate your special show-off events with your siblings. You can divide and share your parents, too. Mom can watch your sister's dance recital while Dad cheers you on at the baseball game.

STEPPARENTS, OR THE MORE THE MERRIER

One of the great advantages to having stepparents is that there are simply *more* parents to go around on V-Day (or any other occasion). The variety of combinations is mind boggling, but it can also be fun. Just remember to keep your sense of humor, and try to keep everyone's name straight when you introduce parents and stepparents to your friends.

WHAT IF NO ONE COMES TO VISIT?

Sometimes *no one* is available to visit you, a heartbreaking situation that is much more serious than having too many parents storm camp at once. Your parents may be out of town on important business, kept at home because of a family problem, or detained by unexpected illness. Sometimes the trusty family car breaks down, or planes and trains are grounded by torrential rain. Anything can happen, so you've got to be prepared emotionally.

If you know in advance that your parents or relatives can't visit on V-Day, tell your counselor. He or she will find an interesting job for you that will help the day go quickly. There are always zillions of things to do that day, and your help will be genuinely appreciated. You can direct cars into camp, greet arriving parents and other dignitaries, help serve food at the big Guest Barbeque, hand out programs at various events, or keep score at a big game. Or you may want to adopt a friend's parents as your unofficial Mom or Dad for the day. (Try to pick someone whose mother always brings the best food).

You can get through V-Day with flying colors if you keep your camp spirits up. Chances are your parents will surprise you with an unofficial visiting-day visit just for you.

Dear Jen,

I'm so sorry about your foot! I hope it's much better by the time you get this letter.

Jenny, guess what? I got a part in the play!! I still can't believe it! I was so scared during tryouts, especially when I had to sing a song all by myself. (The play is an original musical written by the staff.) It's really a bunch of skits about camp life with different words written for familiar songs. I play a new camper who's scared of everything until she tries it. (Great casting, huh?) I know my parents will fall over when they see me on stage!

The best part is that my counselor is the director of the play. Her name is Becky, and she's a drama major at Ohio State—she's so nice, and really funny too. She has a very sophisticated sense of humor. A few girls

I've become friendly with are in the play, too. It's going to take up a lot of time, but I know it will be a great experience.

I'm enclosing some red licorice for you and that revolting purple bubblegum you like so much. I was afraid to mail my Mom's fudge, because it melts pretty fast in the sun. What's up with Greg? Write all.

Love,
Betsy

P.S. We don't have Color War here—but I'm not upset at all.

Dear Betsy,
Thanks for the candy—I really needed it to drown my sorrows. Guess who I saw with his arm around the prettiest counselor in camp? I was destroyed. I guess it was pretty silly thinking he could be interested in me that way, but it still hurt. It happened last week, but I'm pretty much over it now.

My friends here are really great. We talk about boys a lot, because who understands them? There are some pretty cute boys here, but mostly we're just pals. I like playing sports with the boys, and winning—that's really fun. It's a good way to get to know a boy, believe me!

Color War was great! My team won, and we got to go into town and stuff our faces at the ice-cream place.

You won't believe it, but I'm already getting sad that camp will be over soon. Visiting Day was good considering I had two sets of parents to juggle. (You're lucky your original parents are still married to each other—in my bunk that's some kind of a miracle.) Believe it or not, the best part about Visiting Day was that I got my Mom and Dad to talk to each other!

This summer has been really good. All I need to make it perfect is the Best Athlete Award. I can't wait to see you.

Love,
Jenny

AWARDS NIGHT

Before the awards are handed out, Uncle Jay and Aunt Lucy try one last time to revive the old camp spirit. Everybody joins in the singing of the camp alma mater. With arms around each other's shoulders, campers sway back and forth to the melancholy music. If you're not in tears by now, Uncle Jay's speech will surely finish you off. It is designed to make you feel that Camp Anoola just wouldn't be the same without you. Uncle Jay is sure to see the same faces next summer.

For that personalized touch, every camper is given a hollow wooden dowel with a candle in it. One by one campers kneel by the lake, make a wish, and set their candles afloat. After one hundred campers and counselors have made their wishes, the lake is aglow in amber candlelight. This is perhaps the most beautiful sight you'll see all summer! Sure enough, Uncle Jay and Aunt Lucy have succeeded in arousing that old camp spirit, and everyone exchanges hugs and kisses. If you 've been waiting all summer to get close to that special someone, now's the time!) After you've taken everyone's home address, even the addresses of kids you didn't even know went to your camp, it's time for the main event!

Remember your counselor who was also the head of the Arts and Crafts department? Remember all those nights when your cabin was left under the care of a neighboring counselor because your counselor had to attend to some "important business"? And you thought she was running off into the woods to meet her boyfriend. Shame on you! All those sleepless nights your poor counselor spent alone in the arts-and-crafts building constructing the spectacle for this evening's major event—the toilet paper float!

Slowly, from the far end of the lake, a white toilet paper monster emerges. It bobs up and down, up and down, until it's in clear view for all to see. Then with the flick of his wrist, Uncle Jay tosses a candle that lands right in the lake. With another flick of the wrist the flame is tossed and the float ignites! There in orange and blue flames, bigger than life itself, is written "Angola or Bust!" So ends the ceremony and Awards Night officially begins.

Awards Night has a special significance because it means the end of summer and all the happy and sad times you shared with your friends. Awards can be silly or meaningful, but they're always a reminder of what camp meant to you.

Most camps try to give out about 187 awards so that every kid goes home with something. The most prized award is usually the Best Camper Award, although winning this award can present some problems for the honored recipient. Intense feelings of jealousy and envy from all the other campers may lead to some pranks, like hiding the Best Camper's clothes before it's time to get on the bus going home. A smart Best Camper may decide to donate his award to his entire cabin— "A great bunch of kids who made me what I am today."

Here are some typical honors handed out on Awards Night:

Dolphin Award—For the camper who learned the most new tricks in the water.

Freckle-Face Award—For the camper who grew the most new ones.

Fastest-Camper Award—For the camper who ran, swam or hiked the fastest (or for the camper who made out the best with members of the opposite sex).

Pig-Out Award—For the child who consumed more than his body weight in food on All-You-Can-Eat-Night.

Gross-Out Award—For creativity and orginality in the field of disgusting activities.

Good-Sport Award—For the counselor who remained the most cheerful despite pranks, raids, pillow fights and other obnoxious activities from his/her cabinful of angels.

Klutziest-Counselor/Camper Award—A pair of awards for the counselor and camper who broke the most bones, tore the most ligaments, sprained the most muscles, sustained the most bruises, and could always be counted on to slide in the Jell-O during a food fight.

Cockroach Cabin Award—For the bunk that consistently failed inspection with flying colors and grew enough mold to support a family of fungus as well as new forms of flying, crawling creatures.

Uncle Jay and Aunt Lucy Award—For the unfortunate pair who most resemble Uncle Jay and Aunt Lucy, and will probably own a camp in the Berkshires when they grow up.

Bill Murray Meatballs *Memorial Award*—For the nuttiest counselor in camp, who lived up to the motto "Rules were made to be broken!" (Campers select this award recipient.)

Dear Doug,

Does Cindy have a friend for me? All the girls across the lake are terrible. Well, maybe not all—but most. Anyway, too bad about bug juice patrol. Better be careful next time!

It's almost the end of camp, and I'm not ready to go home. I haven't pitched a no-hitter yet. I really want to before the last day. Our big game is coming up. Keep your fingers crossed for me. I better do it, so I can get an award. I know my dad is dying for me to bring one home.

Oh well, enough indoor activity like letter writing. I'm going to practice, since it stopped raining.

Mitch

P.S. Remember I like girls who like baseball.

Dear Jenny,

I can't believe the summer is ending. Everything went so fast once I got the part in the play. I felt great on Visiting Day. Everyone made a big fuss over me. I ate so much food I thought I would burst (my mother brought up enough food for the whole camp. She must have thought they never feed us here).

I'll tell you now—I didn't believe it in June, but I admit it—you were right about camp. I'll never forget it. Last night was our Awards Night, and guess who won Most Improved Swimmer? That's right—me! Of course, considering I could barely float when I came here, it's not surprising that I was the most improved! Did you win your award? I hope so.

I'm really going to miss the kids here, and especially my counselor. I hope when I grow up I can be just like her—maybe I'll even end up a counselor at Na-Sha-Pa. Wouldn't that be funny!

I can't wait to see you and talk about everything we didn't write about. Maybe we can go to the same camp next summer. See you at home.

Love,
Betsy